nd wife team

loney Tree

5.

JP

THE LIBRARY

THE Library

SARAH STEWART

Pictures by
DAVID SMALL

F

FRANCES LINCOLN
CHILDREN'S BOOKS

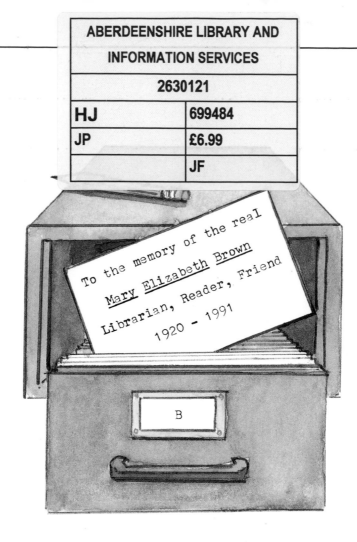

To the memory of the real
<u>Mary Elizabeth Brown</u>
Librarian, Reader, Friend
1920 - 1991

Text copyright © 1995 by Sarah Stewart
Illustrations copyright © 1995 by David Small

First published in the USA in 1995 by Farrar, Straus and Giroux
First published in the UK in 2006 by Frances Lincoln Children's Books
4 Torriano Mews, Torriano Avenue, London NW5 2RZ
www.franceslincoln.com

First paperback edition published in the UK in 2008

British Library Cataloguing in Publication Data
available on request

ISBN: 978-1-84507-607-8

Printed in China

1 3 5 7 9 8 6 4 2

Elizabeth Brown
entered the world
dropping straight down from the sky.

Elizabeth Brown
entered the world
skinny, nearsighted, and shy.

She didn't like to play with dolls,
she didn't like to skate.
She learned to read quite early
and at an incredible rate.

 She always took a book to bed,
with a flashlight under the sheet.
She'd make a tent of covers
and read herself to sleep.

Elizabeth Brown
went off to school
dragging a steamer trunk.

Elizabeth Brown
unpacked her books,
breaking the upper bunk.

She sat in all her classes
and doodled on a pad,
adrift in dreams of entering
a readers' olympiad.

She manufactured library cards
and checked out books to friends,
then shocked them with her midnight raids
to collect the books again.

Elizabeth Brown
preferred a book
to going on a date.

While friends went out
and danced till dawn,
she stayed up reading late.

She took the train one afternoon
and promptly lost her way,
so bought a house and settled down
to tutoring for pay.

Elizabeth Brown
walked into town
summer, fall, winter and spring.

Elizabeth Brown
walked into town
looking for only one thing.

She didn't want potato chips,
she didn't want new clothes.
she went straight to the bookstore.
"May I have one of **those**?"

Elizabeth Brown
walked right back home
and read and read and read.

 She even read while
exercising,
and standing on her head.

She made a list of groceries
and tucked it in a book,
then lost the list among the fruits
and left with nothing to cook.

She read about Greek goddesses
while vacuuming the floor.
Attending only to her book,
she'd walk into a door.

Books were piled on top of chairs
and spread across the floor.
Her shelves began to fall apart,
as she read more and more.

Big books made very solid stacks
on which teacups could rest.
Small books became the building blocks
for busy little guests.

When volumes climbed the parlour walls
and blocked the big front door,
she had to face the awful fact
she could not have one more.

Elizabeth Brown
walked into town
that very afternoon.

Elizabeth Brown
walked into town
whistling a happy tune.

She didn't want a bicycle,
she didn't want silk bows.
She went straight to the courthouse –
"May I have one of **those**?"

The form was for donations.
She quickly wrote this line:
"I, E. Brown, give to the town
all that was ever mine."

Elizabeth Brown
moved in with a friend
and lived to a ripe old age.

They walked to the library
day after day,
and turned page…
after page…

after page.

MORE TITLES
FROM FRANCES LINCOLN CHILDREN'S BOOKS

The Gardener
Sarah Stewart
Illustrated by David Small

Lydia Grace Finch loves writing letters almost as much as
she loves gardening. Armed with her tiny suitcase and a packet
of seeds, she goes to stay with her uncle in the grey city.
Gradually she brings warmth and colour to his bakery, and
to the lives of the people who work there.

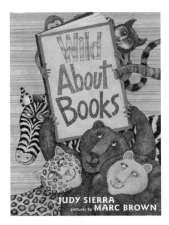

Wild About Books
Judy Sierra
Illustrated by Marc Brown

All the animals are very curious when a mobile library arrives
in the zoo, but soon they can't wait to learn about 'this new
something called reading'. They read thin books and fat books
and Cat in the Hat books. Molly even finds waterproof books for
the otter, who never goes swimming without Harry Potter! Read
along with the book-loving animals and go wild, simply wild
about wonderful books

Once Upon a Time
Niki Daly

Sarie doesn't like school. Every time she has to take out her
reading book, she feels sick, her voice disappears and the other
children tease her. But one person understands how she feels –
Ou Missus, an old lady living across the veld. She tells wonderful
stories, and when Sarie finds a dusty old copy of Cinderella, they
start to read it together.